Teddy Bear Dreams

by Donna Lynne Sava

illustrated by Scott Christian Sava

ipicturebooks

NEW YORK

www.ipicturebooks.com

Distributed by Little, Brown and Company

A heartfelt thank-you to my family for their unceasing love
and support. To my husband, my very best friend . . .
thank you for always believing in me.
And to God for making all of this possible.
—D.L.S.

Teddy Bear Dreams

*An ipicturebook is a book you can read anywhere. Delve into the pages
of the book or download it to your portable, desktop, or handheld PC by
following the directions at "Free ebooks" at www.ipicturebooks.com. Please
have the ISBN number of this book ready to get your free ebook of* Teddy
Bear Dreams. *The ISBN is located above the bar code on the back cover
of this book.*

ipicturebooks.com
24 W. 25th St.
New York, NY 10010
Visit us at *http://www.ipicturebooks.com*

ISBN 1-59019-927-8
LCCN 2001099869

TWP
Printed in Singapore

As he lies in his bed, Teddy thinks of his day;
There was painting and drawing and modeling clay.
Looking up from his pillow, his thoughts start to drift,
From this thing to that thing, and the room starts to shift.
Teddy flies into dreamland, where there's so much to do:
Farming and riding and acting, all the night through.

3...2...1....BLAST OFF!

The rocket sends Teddy up high in the sky,

To look at the world as it goes by.

He sets up his equipment to study in space;

His suit keeps him comfy and covers his face.

As he orbits the earth, he floats to and fro,

And looks at the moon, which has such a bright glow.

DING, DING!

rings the door, and Teddy's first patient walks in.

His face is quite pale and he looks very thin.

He's got a bad runny nose, and a cough, and a sneeze.

Teddy takes out a bottle: "Now take two of these.

In the morning, I know how much better you'll feel;

Now go home and rest so that you will heal."

Cock-a-doodle-doo!

Each day Teddy wakes with the rooster that crows,

Eats a large breakfast, and then off he goes.

First he milks all the cows, and gets every drop,

Then feeds the chickens or harvests a crop.

Today Teddy goes to the fair at sunrise:

"My giant tomato has won the first prize!"

"ACTION!"

snaps the director, and the cameras all roll.

Becoming a star is Teddy's one goal.

He works on his lines late into the night,

He learns every word, and says them just right.

Soon the audience loves him up on the screen,

And on TV, on posters—wherever he's seen.

Clang, CLANG, clang!

Fireman Teddy is trained to help all those in need—
That's the fireman's job and his unspoken creed.
He arrives on the scene and wastes no time at all.
Soon the kitten is saved from a very high fall.
The crowd starts to cheer, "Hip-hip-hooray!"
As Teddy jumps on his truck and gets on his way.

SWOOSH!

With Super-Teddy strength our hero fights crime,
Or rescues people in the nick of time.
He flies through the sky, high over the town;
A swimmer is struggling: "I won't let him drown."
"You saved me, Super-Teddy! Oh, what can I say?"
"Your safety is my thanks, now have a nice day."

Choo, choooooooooo

sounds the train as it starts down the track,

And Engineer Teddy doesn't look back.

Over mountains and bridges, through towns big and small,

His train carries people and packages for all.

It's a long trip across our great nation.

Teddy smiles as he reaches the last destination.

Yee-HAW!

Cowboy Teddy rides the range every day.

He guides the cattle and shows them the way.

If a small calf gets lost out on the trail,

Teddy goes looking, and finds her without fail.

That's the cowboy's job—keep the cattle in sight,

And bring them back safe each and every night.

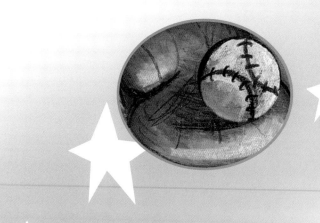

"BATter UP!"

shouts the umpire and the game gets under way.

Teddy's out in the field and ready to play.

He catches the ball as all the fans shout,

Then throws the ball home, and the ump yells, "You're out!"

No score in the ninth, and they cheer Teddy's name.

Crack goes the bat, and Teddy's won the big game!

Clank, Clank!

goes the armor of the king's bravest knight.

Brave Teddy searches for wrongs to make right.

When a dragon swoops in and takes the maiden so fair,

The king sends Knight Teddy off to its lair.

Blow after blow they fight a great fight,

And the maiden is rescued: "Oh, my shining knight!"

"WELCOME
to the BIG top!"

calls Ringmaster Teddy!
Here come the tigers and lions—he's ready.
With a wave of his hand and a stern shout,
He soon has the big cats running about.
The crowd cheers as the animals do their acts with ease,
Jumping through hoops and swinging on the trapeze.

"Land HO!"

Teddy's a pirate, sailing the sea.

No school or parents—it's great to be free.

He has a map, and "X" marks the spot,

Way off on an island where the weather is hot.

He anchors the ship and rows in to shore,

With hopes of finding gold, silver, and more.

As the sun fills the sky, Teddy wakes with a grin.
His dreaming is done now, a new day will begin.
He explores and he learns, growing bigger each day,
And dreams of places and people at work and at play.
The adventures in dreamland allow us to see,
You can do anything you want, if you only believe!